FAIRY TALE PHONICS

DOT AND THE MAGIC POT

A TALE OF WORD FAMILIES

by Rebecca Donnelly
illustrated by Carissa Harris

GRASSHOPPER

Tools for Parents & Teachers

Grasshopper Books enhance imagination and introduce the earliest readers to fiction with fun storylines and illustrations. The easy-to-read text supports early reading experiences with repetitive sentence patterns and sight words.

Before Reading

- Discuss the cover illustration. What do readers see?
- Look at the picture glossary together. Discuss the words.

Read the Book

- Read the book to the child, or have him or her read independently.
- "Walk" through the book and look at the illustrations. Who is the main character? What is happening in the story?

After Reading

- Prompt the child to think more. Ask: Word families are groups of words that end the same and rhyme. What word families did you see in this book? Can you name and spell words in the "-an" word family?

Grasshopper Books are published by Jump!
5357 Penn Avenue South
Minneapolis, MN 55419
www.jumplibrary.com

Library of Congress Cataloging-in-Publication Data

Names: Donnelly, Rebecca, author.
Harris, Carissa, illustrator.
Title: Dot and the magic pot: a tale of word families by Rebecca Donnelly; illustrated by Carissa Harris.
Description: Minneapolis, MN: Jump!, Inc., [2023]
Series: Fairy tale phonics | Includes index.
Audience: Ages 5-8.
Identifiers: LCCN 2022030004 (print)
LCCN 2022030005 (ebook)
ISBN 9798885242721 (hardcover)
ISBN 9798885242738 (paperback)
ISBN 9798885242745 (ebook)
Subjects: LCSH: Readers (Primary)
LCGFT: Readers (Publications)
Classification: LCC PE1119.2 .D6732 2023 (print)
LCC PE1119.2 (ebook)
DDC 428.6/2—dc23/eng/20220719
LC record available at https://lccn.loc.gov/2022030004
LC ebook record available at https://lccn.loc.gov/2022030005

Editor: Eliza Leahy
Direction and Layout: Anna Peterson
Illustrator: Carissa Harris

Printed in the United States of America at Corporate Graphics in North Mankato, Minnesota.

Table of Contents

In This Book:

You will find word families. A word family is a group of words that end the same and rhyme. This story has many word families. Can you find the word family on each page?

Hint: One example of a word family is: **frog**, **bog**, and **log**. See if you can spot these words!

The Pot that Made a Lot

Dot is hungry.

She wants to eat a lot.

But there is no food
in her kitchen.

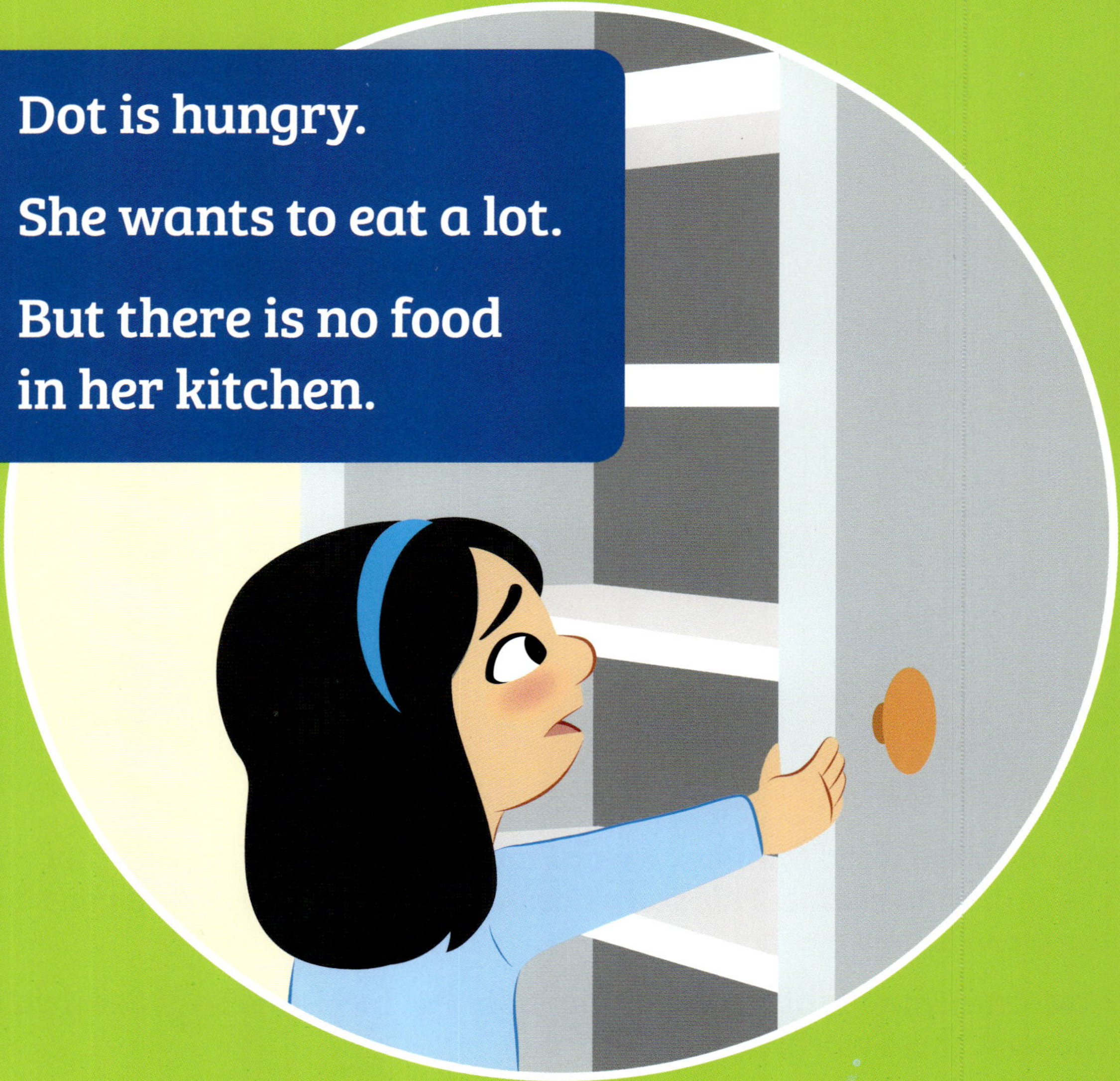

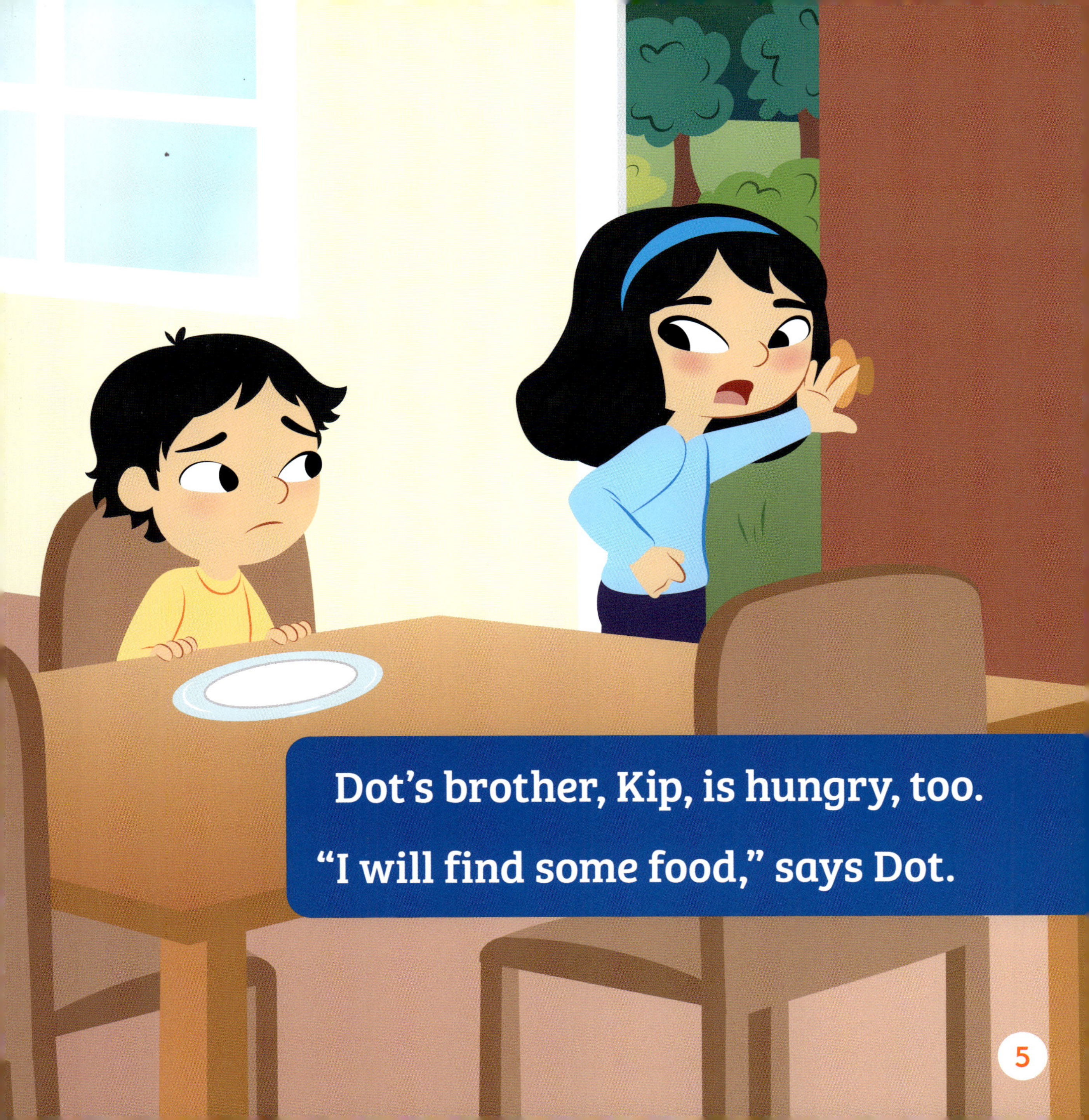

Dot’s brother, Kip, is hungry, too.

“I will find some food,” says Dot.

Dot *sees* a frog in a bog sitting on a log.

"I am hungry," says Dot.

"This is a magic pot," says the frog. "It will make delicious food."

bog

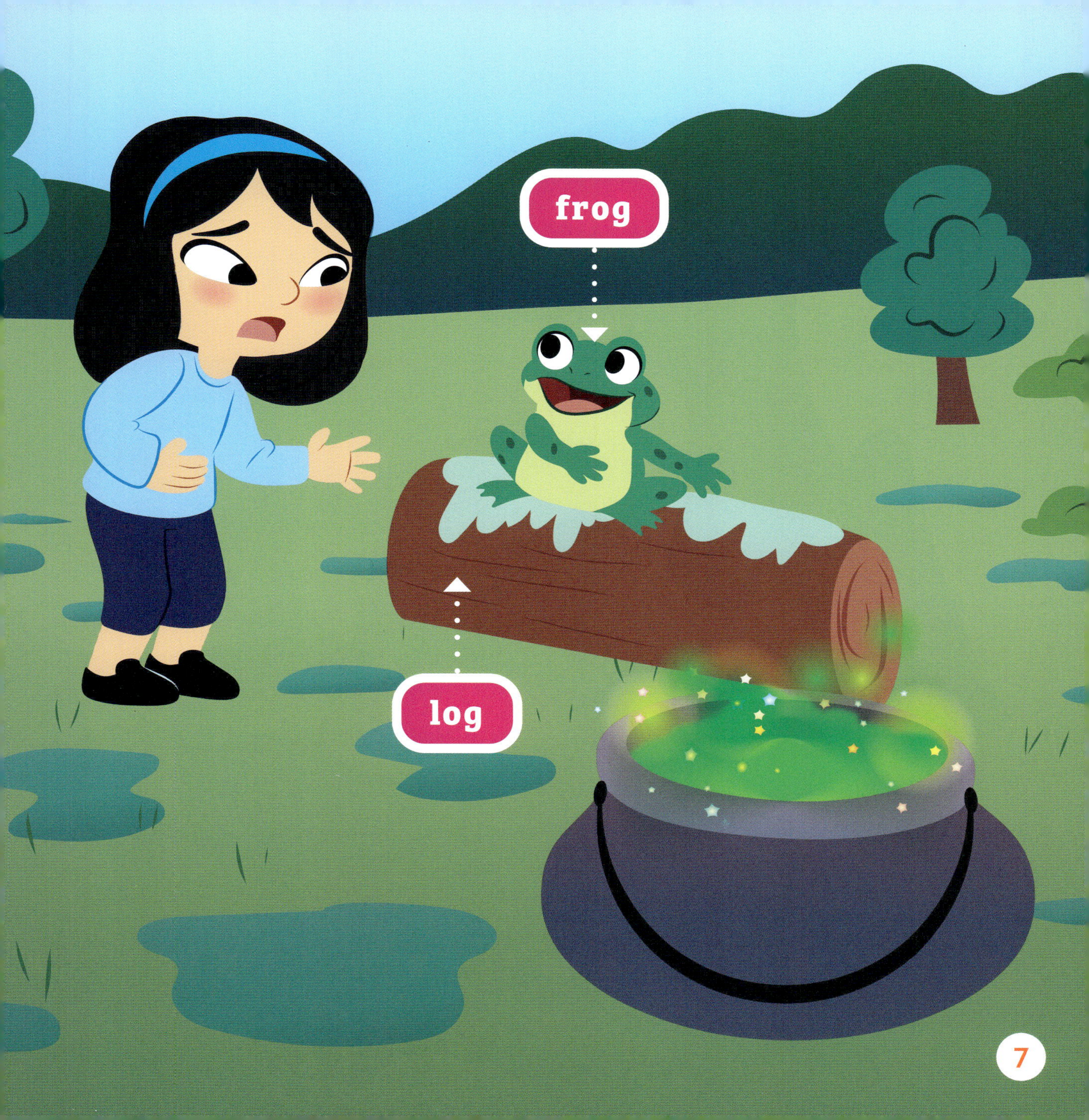
frog
log

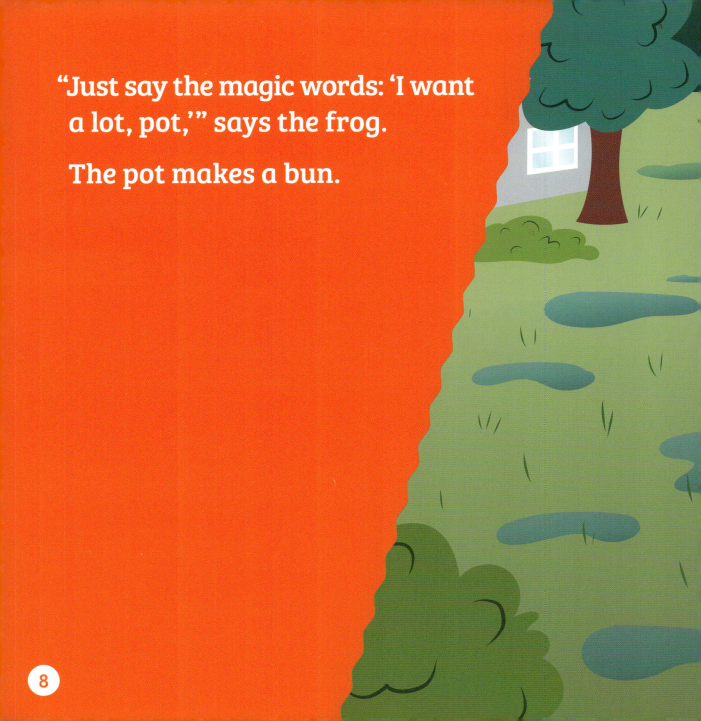

"Just say the magic words: 'I want a lot, pot,'" says the frog.

The pot makes a bun.

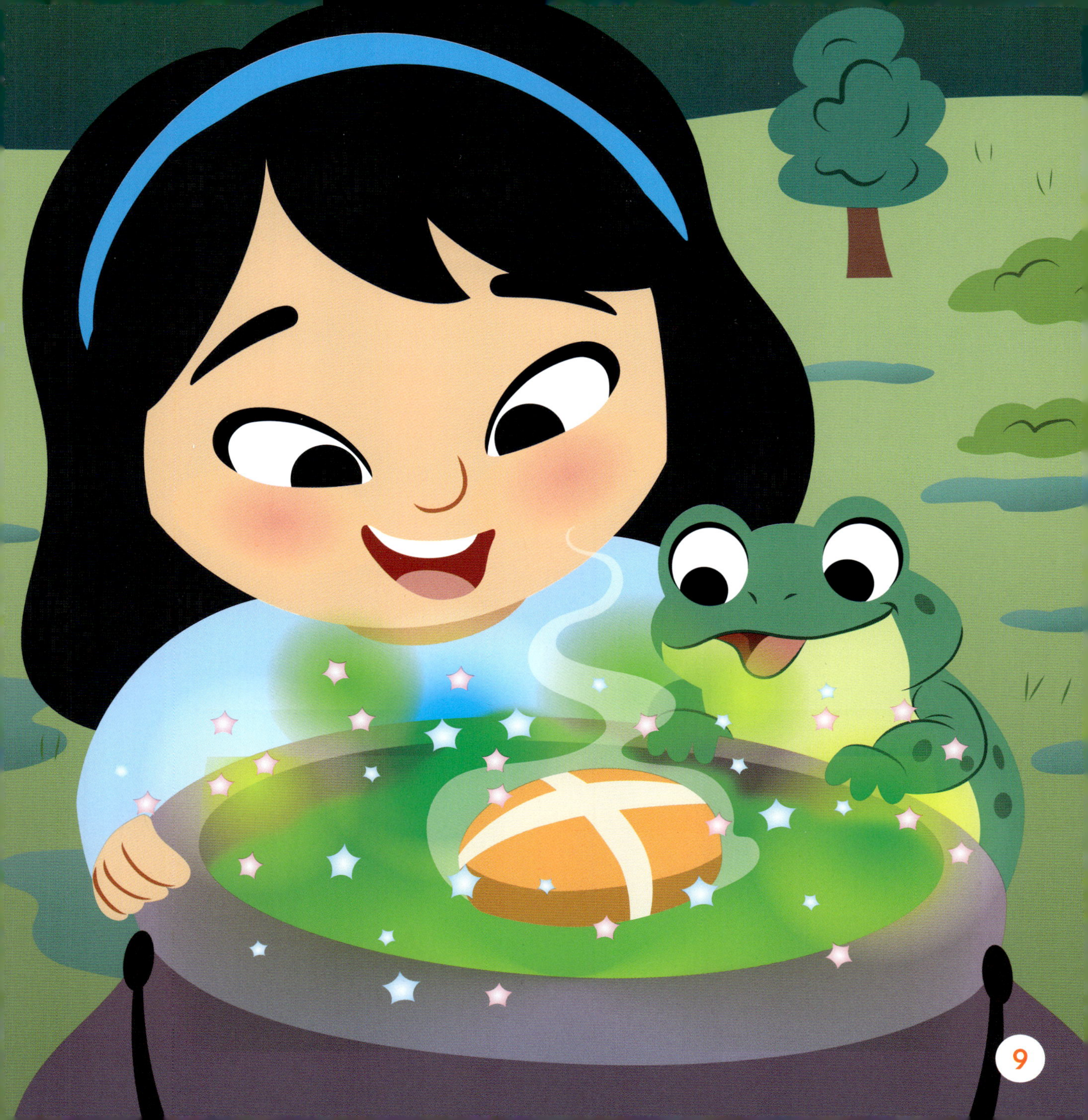

“How fun!” says Dot. “I’ll eat this bun in the sun.”

“You must share,” says the frog. “If not, the pot will stop.”

“I will,” says Dot.

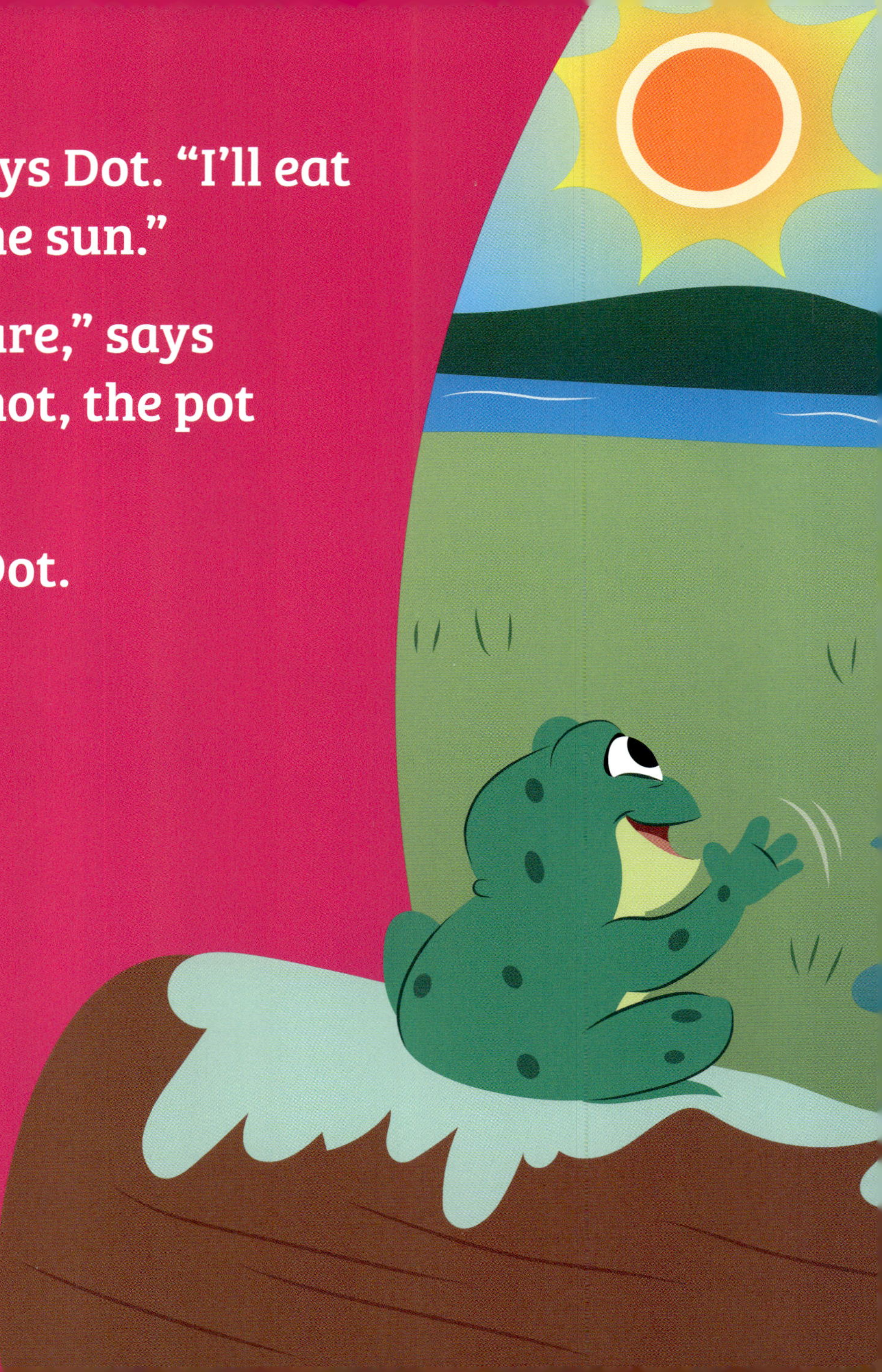

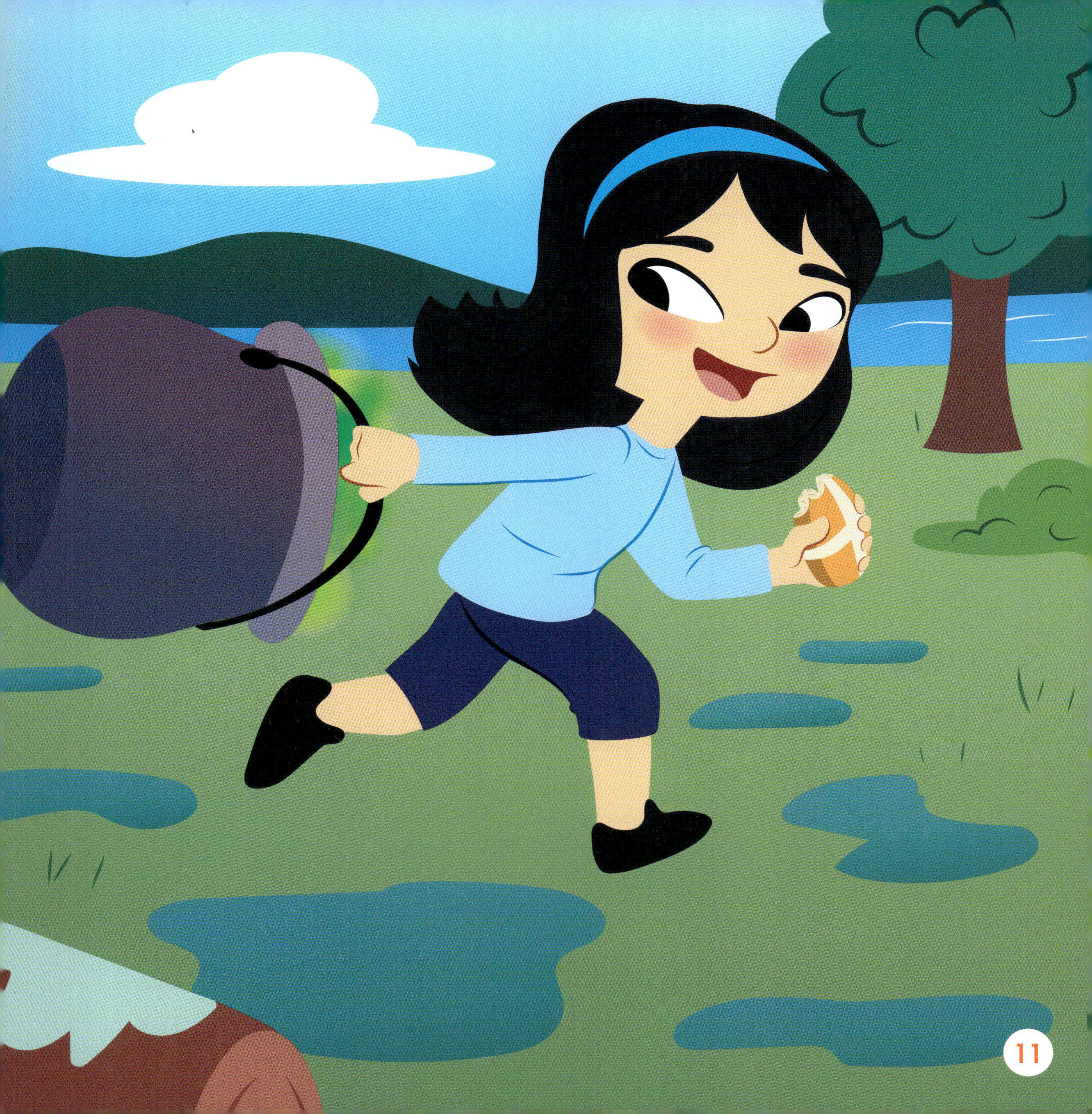

After she eats the bun, Dot goes home.

“I want a lot, pot,” she says.

The pot makes a yam. Then it makes ham and jam!

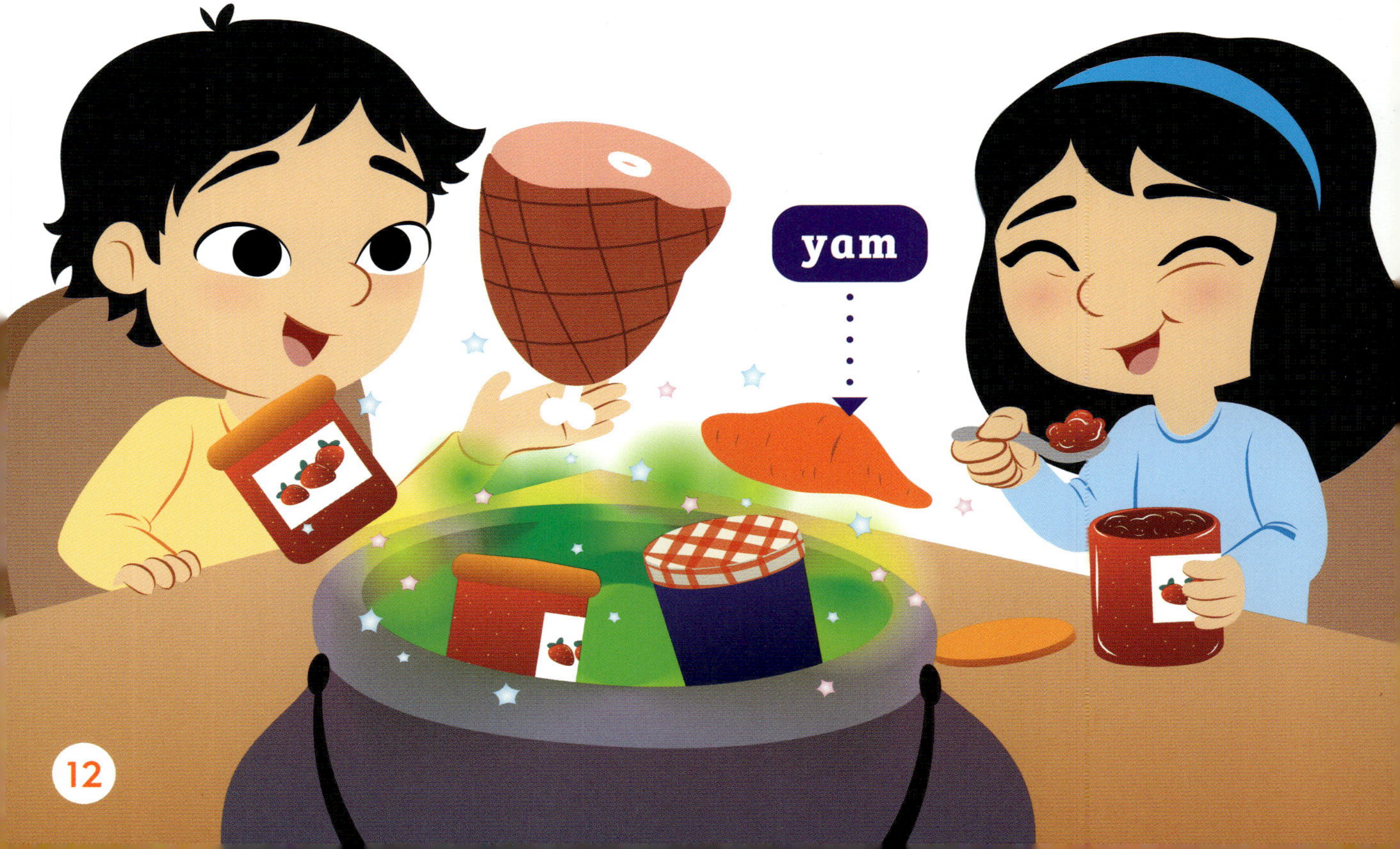
yam

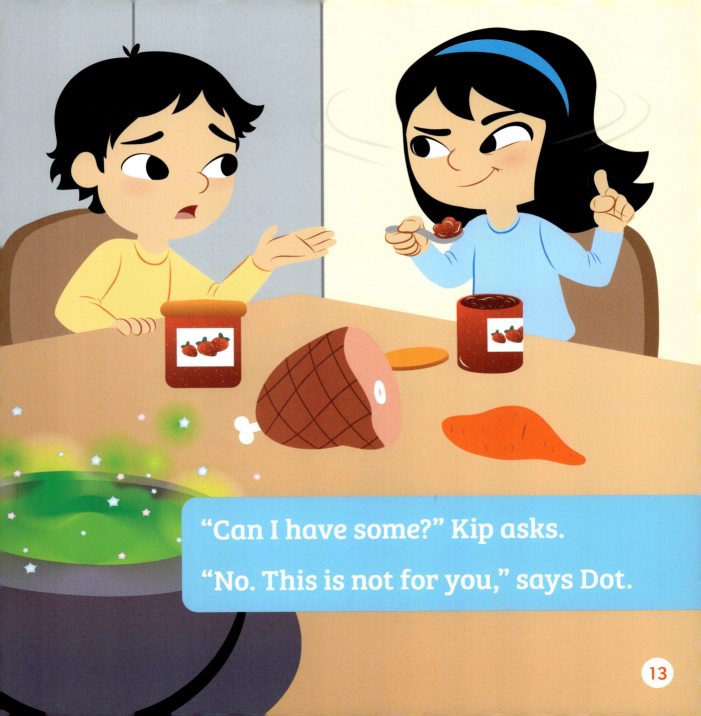

"Can I have some?" Kip asks.

"No. This is not for you," says Dot.

"I want a lot, pot," says Dot.

The pot makes figs
and a very big pig.

Then a wig appears.

"A wig is not food!"
Dot complains.

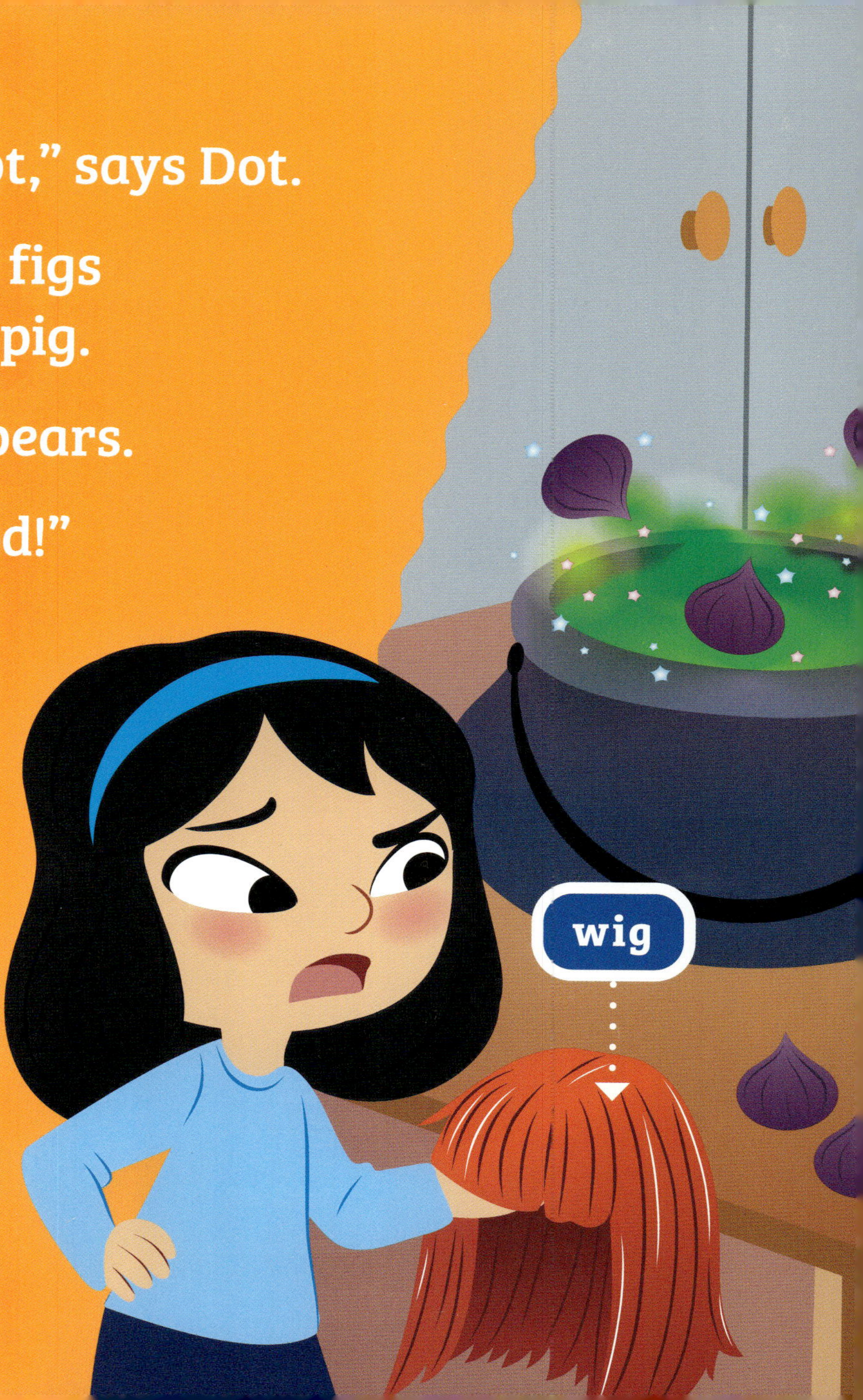
wig

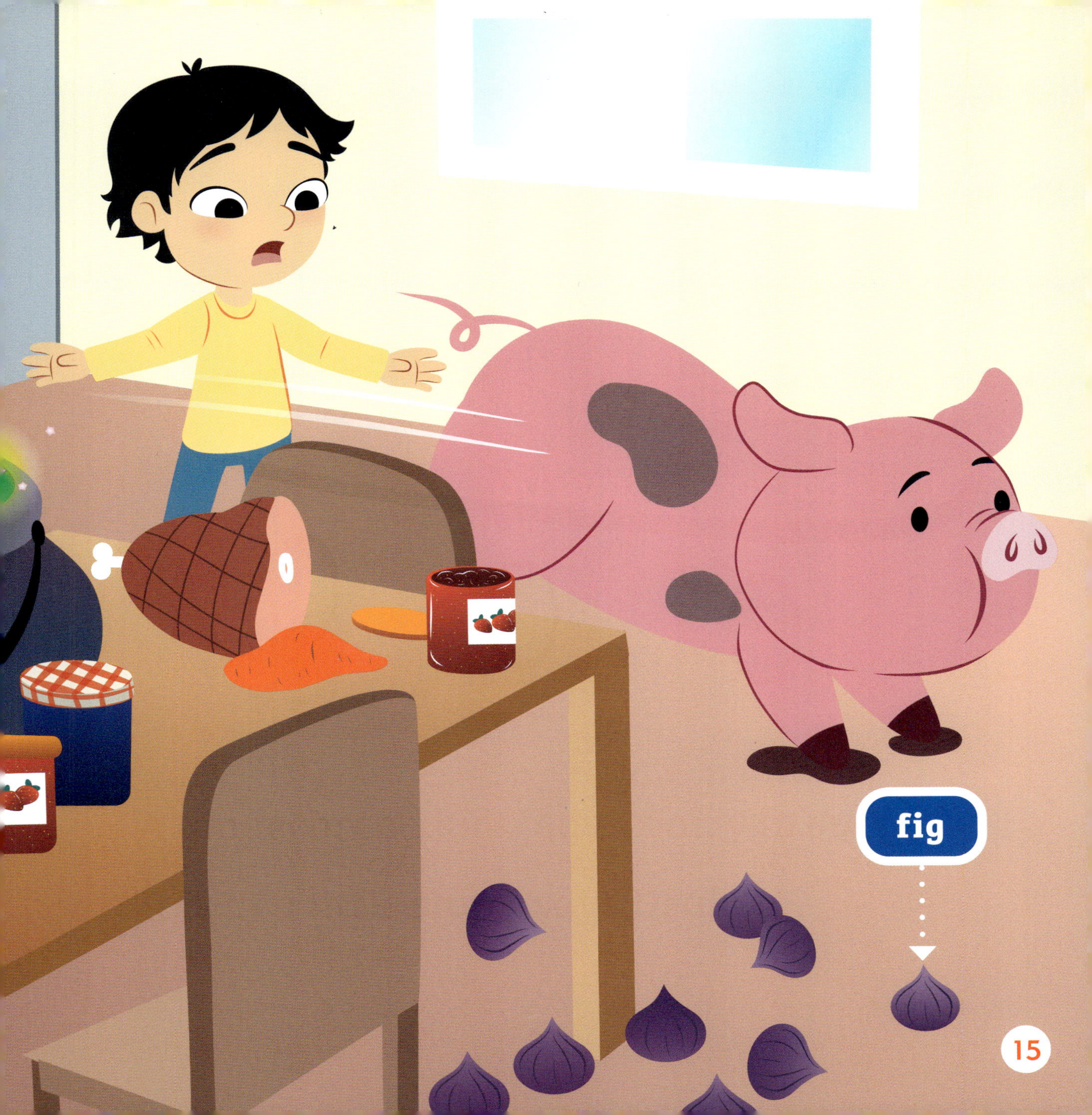
fig

Dot tries again. "I want a lot, pot," she says.

The pot makes a fox and a box.

Then it makes an ox!

"This is not food!" says Dot.

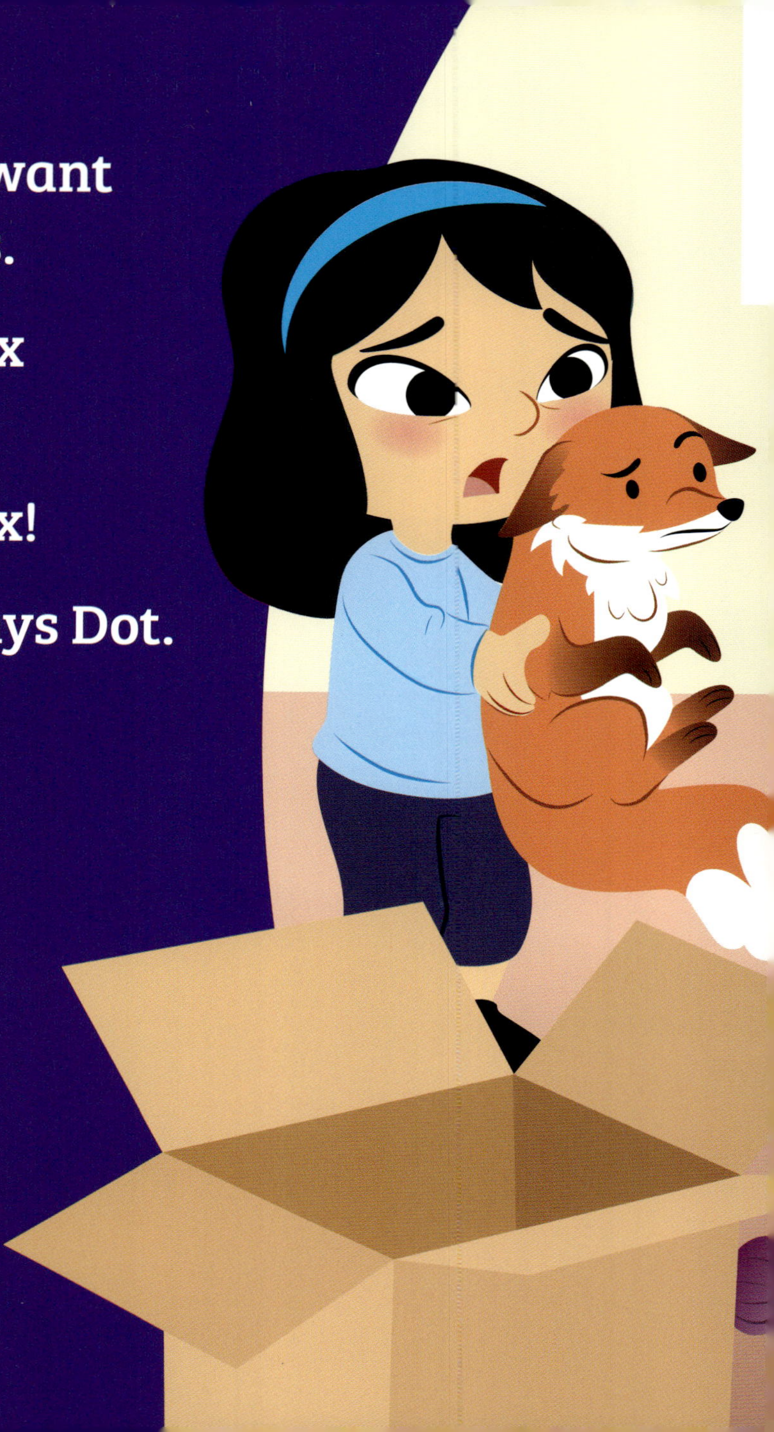

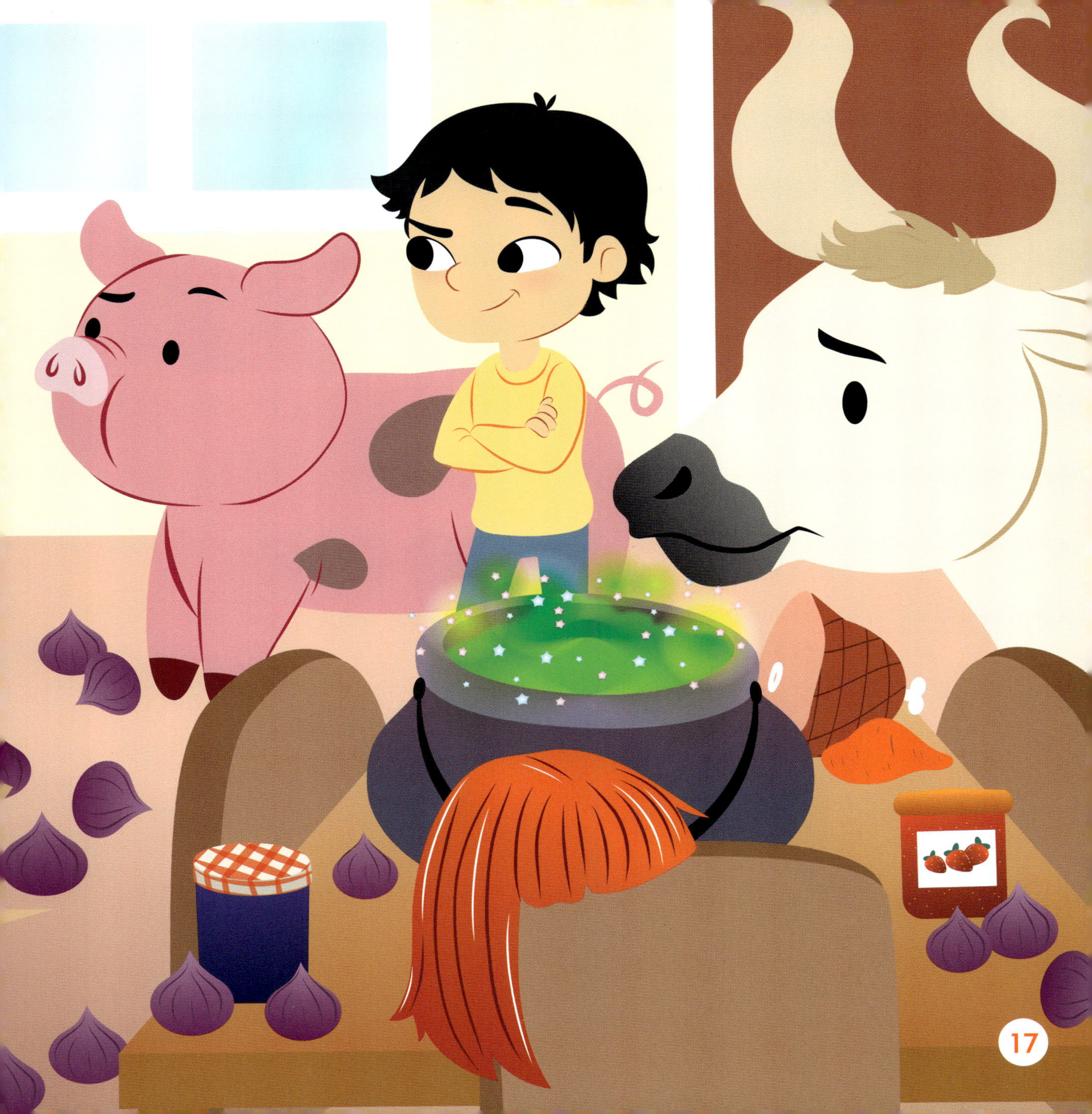

“I want a lot, pot,” says Dot.

The pot makes a hat, a rat, and a mat.

“That is not food either!” says Dot.

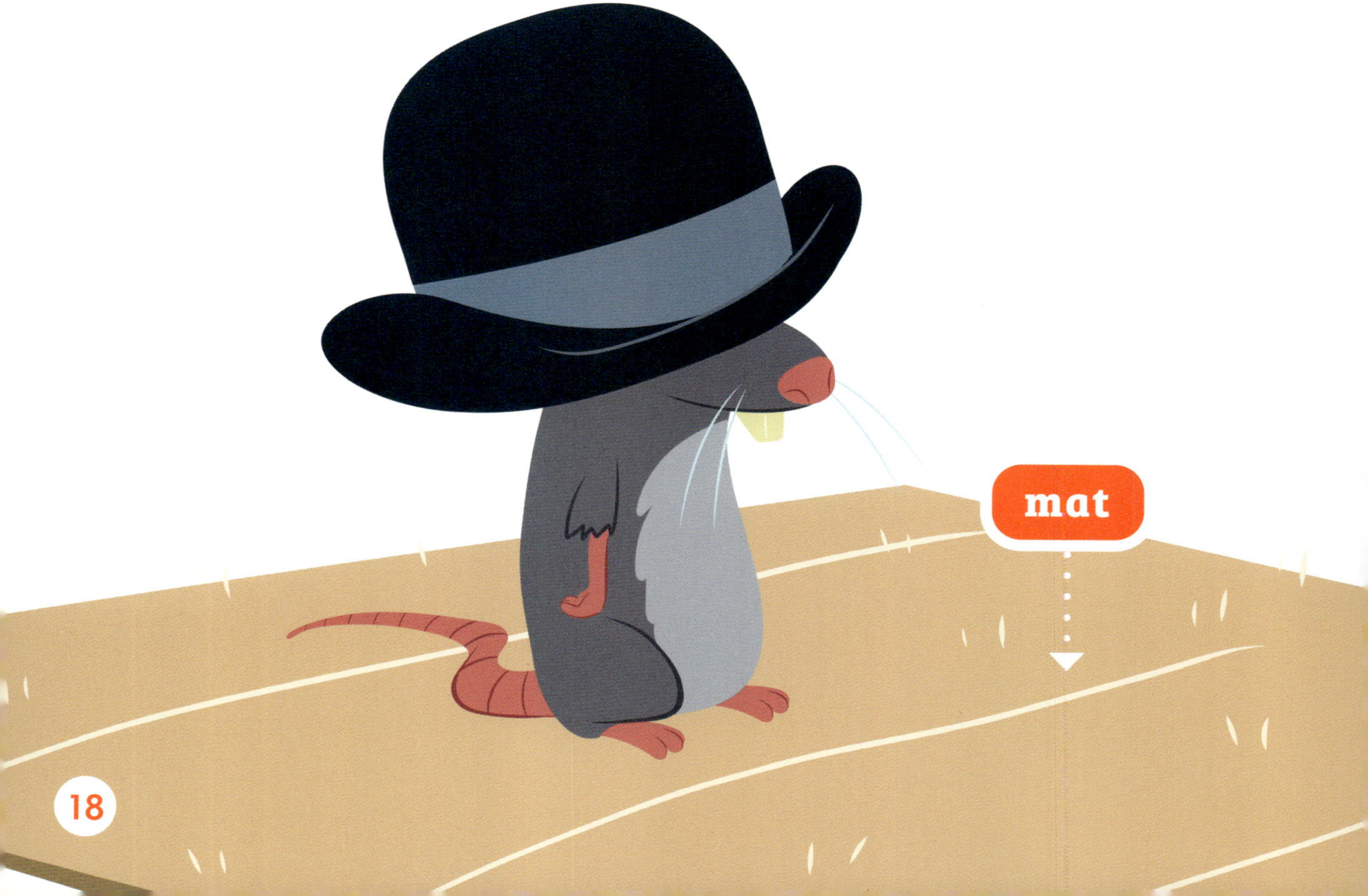
mat

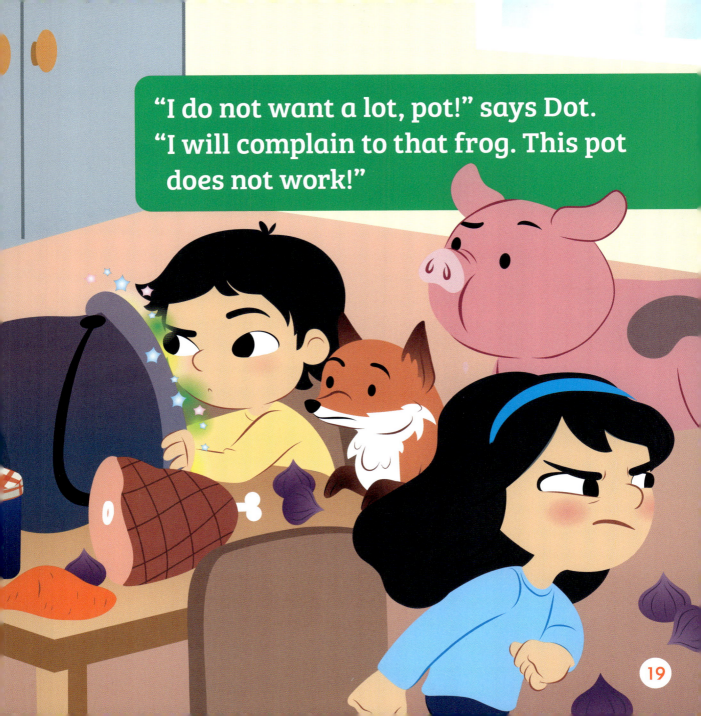

"I do not want a lot, pot!" says Dot. "I will complain to that frog. This pot does not work!"

19

"I want a lot, pot," says Kip.

The pot makes a giant chip and dip.

Dot turns around.

"Would you like some chip?" asks Kip.

"Yes, please!" says Dot.

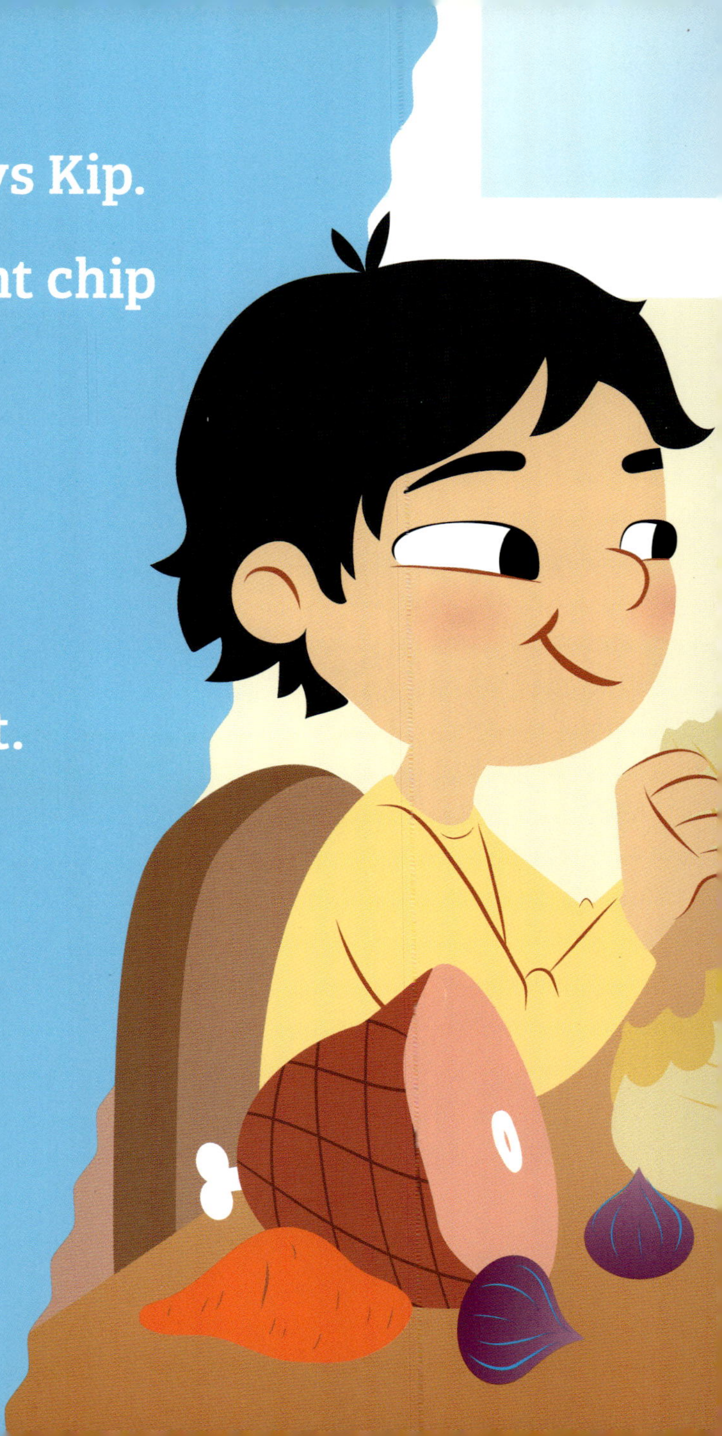

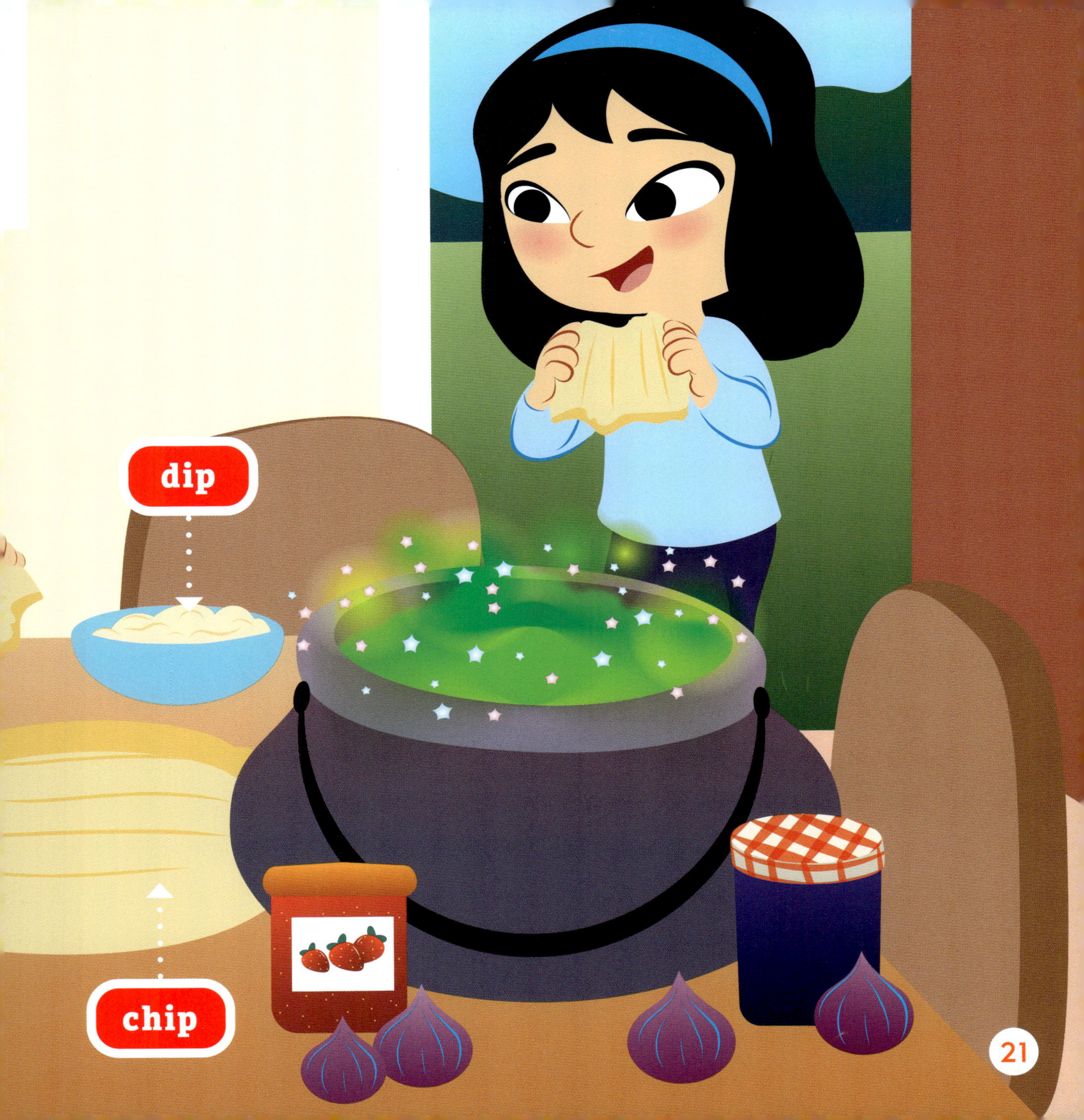
dip
chip

Let's Review!

Hat, **r**at, and **m**at are in the "-at" word family. Point to the words below that are in the "-ig" word family.

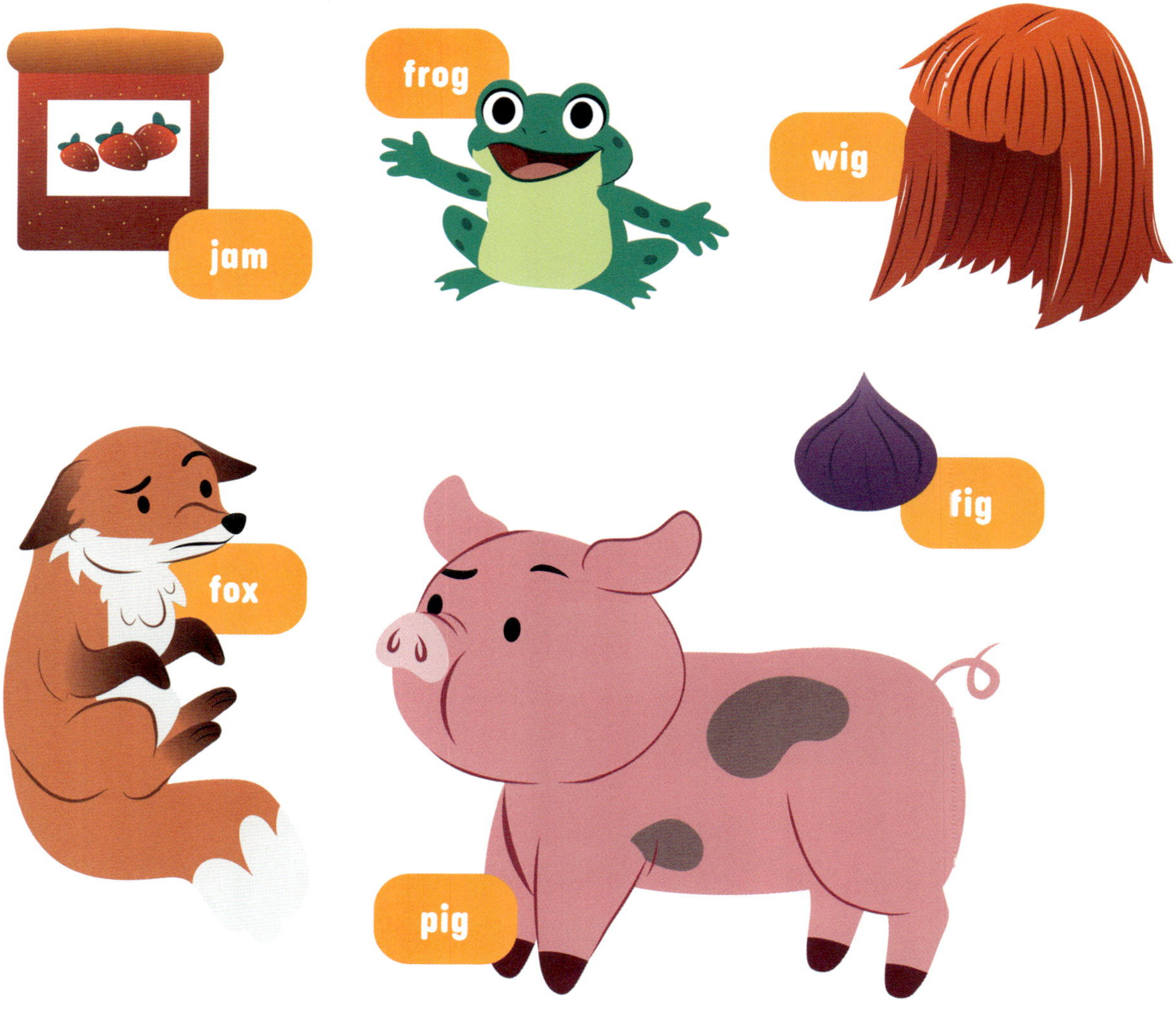
jam
frog
wig
fox
fig
pig

Picture Glossary

appears
Comes into view.

bog
An area of soft, wet land.

complains
Expresses frustration.

delicious
Tasting or smelling very good.

magic
Having the power to make impossible things happen.

share
To divide something between two or more people.

Index

To Learn More

FACT SURFER

Finding more information is as easy as 1, 2, 3.

❶ Go to www.factsurfer.com

❷ Enter "**Dotandthemagicpot**" into the search box.

❸ Choose your book to see a list of websites.